# The Great Vacation

### By: Marsha Mims-Word

*Illustrated By: Christina Halcie Seay*

To order additional copies of this book, contact:
Xlibris
1-888-795-4274
www.Xlibris.com
Orders@Xlibris.com

# Dedication

This book is dedicated to my husband and three sons
for your love and support.

My name is John Alonzo, Jr. but my family calls me AJ. My Mom liked the name AJ and decided to flip the initials of my first and middle names; and that's how my family began calling me AJ. I am the middle child; I am six years old; my brother Andre is twelve and the baby of the family, Alex, is three years old.

My Dad is a middle school principal and this year school ended early in June. So he decided it was time for us to begin bonding like real men with a road trip. It was a sunny June day when my Dad, two brothers and I began packing our jeep for what would be the first vacation for the "Word" men.

We piled blankets, pillows and lots of snacks for our adventure into my Dad's black jeep Cherokee. Only men allowed on this trip; on our own for three whole weeks. This was going to be so much fun.

The night before our trip, Mom and Dad sat down to map out our route. The first stop was the beach, Nags Head, North Carolina; then onto Kingstree, South Carolina, my Grandma's home town. From South Carolina, we would travel to Halifax, Virginia, my Granddad's home town. After Halifax the journey would take us to Williamsburg, Virginia for more fun. As my parents planned this trip, I could hardly contain myself. Sleep was going to be very hard that night. Our final two stops on this journey were Hampton and Newport News, Virginia, to visit my cousins. WHOOPIE, WHAT BIG FUN WE WERE GOING TO HAVE.

That morning we rose pretty early to do the final packing of our belongings for the next three weeks. My job was to take care of my little brother Alex, Andre was in charge of reading the map and Dad was the captain of the jeep. We were on our way.

Six hours later and several rest stops, we arrived in Nags Head, North Carolina. I helped watch Alex while Dad checked us into our room at the Embassy Suites.

Our first activity was the beach. We changed into our swim trunks and hit the ocean. We built sand castles, buried Dad a couple of times and collected shells. The water felt great. It was a hot June day and the ocean water cooled us.

Later that day we visited the Wright Brothers Museum and saw their plane. It was a funny plane; amazing that the thing ever made it off the ground. This was a lot different from the planes I have flown on.

It was time for dinner, baths and bed. We had one more day in Nags Head before we journey to South Carolina to see Aunt Lilla Mae.

We rose early to begin our next venture. We packed the jeep and headed further south to Kingstree, South Carolina, about 40 miles from Florence, South Carolina.

When we arrived, Aunt Lilla Mae was so excited to see us. She cooked us a wonderful lunch of fried chicken and homemade biscuits. I stuffed myself. We then hit the streets of Kingstree to walk off some of the lunch but to also do some exploring.

This is a small town. Not many traffic lights, no major shopping malls or video arcades. But we still found plenty to do. We stopped to see Uncle Van; he is my Grandma's brother. He owns lots of pigs. We had fun watching the pigs run through the yard and eating their food. Boy, they sure can pack away food.

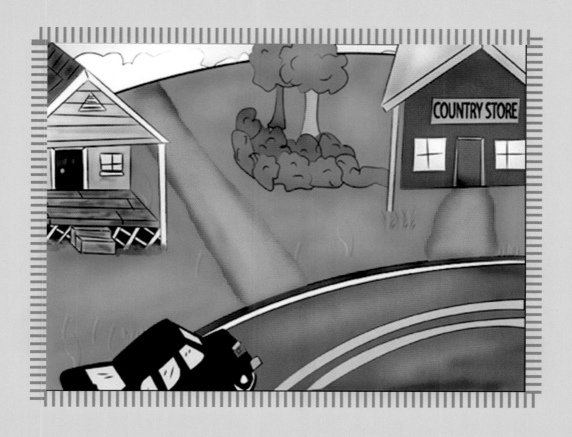

Dad took us to see the house my Grandma grew up in and the little country store her Dad owned. It was nice to learn so much family history. This was another fun filled day. We headed back to Aunt Lilla Mae's for another amazing meal.

We decided to all sleep in the same room that night and talk about what we have enjoyed so far on the trip. I enjoyed seeing the pigs, Alex liked climbing the tree in Aunt Lilla Mae's yard and Andre liked helping Dad navigate the trip. Dad just liked us being together. We had one more day in South Carolina then we were heading to Halifax Virginia, the hometown of Aunt Bell, my Granddad's sister.

On the third morning of our visit, we left South Carolina and traveled
to Halifax Virginia. We arrived eight hours later. Wow what a ride.
Alex and I slept most of this journey. Aunt Bell had pigs, chickens, a
huge vegetable garden and lots of dogs. I don't think all the dogs
belonged to her, they just liked hanging around her house.

Again, we ate very well; lots of homemade food, finger licking good.

Dad decided it was time to do the laundry since this was our second week on the road. We found a laundromat in town. While we were washing our clothes, Alex found a couple of pennies. He asked Dad if he could use his pennies to buy a soda from the machine. Dad told him no because he did not have enough money and besides, pennies do not work in the soda machine.

Well, Alex being a three year old and not understanding why pennies would not work in the soda machine, decided to put one of his pennies into the machine and hit the Mountain Dew tab. Well guess what, Alex hit the jackpot. Mountain Dews started coming out of the machine and would not stop. We collected 72 sodas. When we left, sodas were still shooting out of the machine. This was unbelievable; all of this soda due to my little brother inserting one penny into the machine. We had Mountain Dews for the remaining trip.

We went back to Aunt Bell's, left her with Mountain Dews and headed to our next stop, Williamsburg, Virginia and Busch Gardens. Six hours later, we arrived in Williamsburg and checked into the Days Inn.

It was time to go for a swim. We all raced to the room, changed and spent the next two hours poolside. Two hours in the water can work up a large appetite.

We headed to Pizza Hut for dinner. We all ate till we could not move. We drove back to our room for baths and a little down time before lights out.

The next day, we were off to Williamsburg, the Old Country. It was interesting to see all the workers dressed in colonial costumes. That was fun.

Later that day, we arrived at Busch Gardens. All the rides were wonderful. We rode the water log canoe. Everyone in the canoe got wet when the canoe flew down a large hill. We left the park at dark and back to our hotel room to pack for our early morning departure to Hampton Virginia.

We arrived in Hampton the next day at our cousin JoAnn's house. She is Grandma's niece. She has five children, all are older than me and Alex with the exception of her youngest daughter, who is the same age as Alex.

We ate a hardy breakfast and played with their dog. I believe it was a German Shepard; real friendly animal.

Dad took us to Hampton University for a tour. This is where cousin JoAnn use to work. She is now the president of Langston University in Oklahoma.

After our day in Hampton, we packed the jeep and departed to our final stop of this journey. Newport News Virginia, cousin Sue's house. Cousin Sue is Grandma's niece and sister to cousin JoAnn. Sue has a daughter named Ingrid.

Again we had a wonderful meal. I thought to myself, if I don't remember anything about this trip, I will definitely remember the terrific meals we had with our relatives from the South.

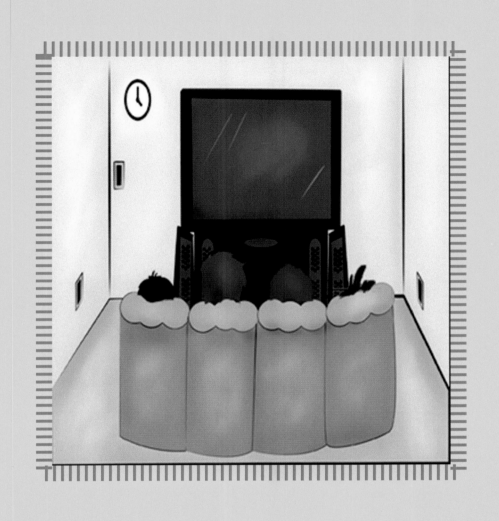

We watched television, played football in the yard at cousin Sue's, just a day of relaxation before our trip home.

I really was looking forward to returning home, seeing Mom and our dog Fluff. Fluff is a chow chow. It had been three weeks, while we talked to Mom on the telephone at every stop; I looked forward to seeing her. I guess I was getting a little homesick. We spent the night at cousin Sue's. The next day we left early to avoid traffic coming into Washington, DC.

At last, we returned home. I saw my house a block away. Mom and Fluff were standing in the door. I could not wait to sit down and play with Fluff and tell Mom all about my three weeks with my Dad and two brothers. I enjoyed every moment of our bonding as "Word" men. I guess Dad plan worked; the purpose of our trip was to bring us closer together. This trip did just that.

Printed in the United States
By Bookmasters